CARRIE SHOOK

Direct Sales Consultant

847-708-1530 phone

847-579-0096 fax

cshook29@yahoo.com

Five Town

WRITTEN BY NADIA HIGGINS • ILLUSTRATED BY RONNIE ROONEY

The Child's World

Published by The Child's World®
1980 Lookout Drive • Mankato, MN 56003-1705
800-599-READ • www.childsworld.com

ACKNOWLEDGMENTS
The Child's World®: Mary Berendes, Publishing Director
The Design Lab: Design and production
Red Line Editorial: Editorial direction

LIBRARY OF CONGRESS CATALOGING-IN-PUBLICATION DATA
Higgins, Nadia.
 Five town / written by Nadia Higgins ;
illustrated by Ronnie Rooney.
   p. cm.
 ISBN 978-1-60253-498-8 (lib. bd. : alk. paper)
1. Five (The number)—Juvenile literature. 2. Number concept—
Juvenile literature. I. Rooney, Ronnie, ill. II. Title. III. Title: 5 town.
 QA141.3.H573 2010
 513.2—dc22   2010007539

Printed in the United States of America in Mankato, Minnesota.
July 2010
F11538

About the Author

Nadia Higgins is a children's book writer in Minneapolis, Minnesota. She owns 1 wedding ring, 2 pairs of sneakers, and 7 plants. Her favorite time of day is 4 in the afternoon. That's when she gets to play Crazy Eights and other games with her 2 kids.

About the Illustrator

Ronnie Rooney was born and raised in Massachusetts. She attended the University of Massachusetts at Amherst for her undergraduate study and Savannah College of Art and Design for her MFA in illustration. Ronnie has illustrated numerous books for children. She hopes to pass this love of art on to her daughter.

The **5**s are thrilled about their **five**-fingered hands. How do they greet each other in **Five** Town? They say, "Give me **five**!"

And isn't it great that toes come in **fives**, too? The **5**s sure think so.

That's why they love to wear flip-flops—even in winter.

5

five

The **5**s of **Five** Town think **five** is the nicest number around.

Today, fluffy clouds drift in the sky. "What do you see?" Fern **5** asks her brother, Fred **5**. They gaze for **five** hours. They are delighted by what they find!

11

Meanwhile, Finn **5** is making a sandwich. It's his favorite: peanut butter, jelly, honey, and banana . . . with a pickle on top.

13

Fran **5** has one nickel.

What will she buy?

A book, a bike, or a bed?

In **Five** Town, everything

costs only **five** cents!

That's it! Fran sees the perfect thing—
a star!

Fran and Fern meet at the diner. They each eat **five** slices of pizza and drink **five** milkshakes.

No wonder their tummies are round!

19

After **five** movies, the
friends head for home.
"Good night, good night,
good night, good night,
good night," they say.
It's been another *five*-ulous
day in **Five** Town!

21

What Makes Five?

Cover one picture with your hand. How many are left? What number goes with 1 to make 5?

How many will be left if you cover four pictures?

Cover two pictures with your hand. Count how many are left. What number goes with 2 to make 5?

How many will be left if you cover three pictures?

Know Your Numbers

Hola, 5!

How do you say "five" in Spanish? Cinco. Say it: *SING-koh*.

Five on Stage

The 5s are delighted to go see a quintet perform. That happens when five musicians play together.

Favorite Shape

Have you ever heard of a pentagon? That's a 5's favorite shape. It has five sides and five corners.

Favorite Sport

Why do 5s love basketball most of all? Because five players make a team!

Take Five

What does a 5 do when he's tired of something? He "takes five." That's an expression that means to take a short break—maybe a five-minute break!

Find Five

Can you find all the things that come in fives in this book? How many groups of five are there?